Grover's Just So-So Stories

How the Monster Got His Fur & How the Honker Got His Honk

By Nancy Hall

Illustrated by Rick Wetzel

Featuring Jim Henson's Sesame Street Muppets

A Sesame Street/Golden Press Book

Published by Western Publishing Company, Inc., in conjunction

with Children's Television Workshop.

Library of Congress Catalog Card Number: 87-82028 ISBN: 0-307-23160-7

How the Monster Got His Fur

Hello, everybodee. This is lovable, furry old Grover here to tell you how some of your favorite friends on Sesame Street got to be the very special ways they are today.

First I will tell you the story of how the monsters got fur. This is one of my particular favorites.

Monsters did not always have beautiful, colorful, furry fur. In the very beginning, before you and I were even born, none of the monsters had any fur at all. They did not have nice comfy homes to live in, either.

Now, this was just fine in the spring and the summer, and even in the early fall. But by the time winter came, the monsters got very cold.

Well, one winter the monsters all got together and came up with a plan. They would cover themselves with fur, and they would not be cold anymore.

So they went to Hooper's Trading Post.

PICKLE

Choosing the kind of fur they were going to wear was a very big decision. There were short furs and long furs and red furs and purple furs and orange furs and blue furs and every other kind of fur. One by one, everybody tried on a lovely cozy-warm suit of fur.

I am ashamed to tell you this, but way back in the very beginning, monsters were not sweet and thoughtful like they are today. In fact, they sometimes liked to scare people and do naughty things.

So the monsters chose the shaggiest, scariest fur they could find. And then they tried to scare their friends.

But guess what! The monsters did not look scary at all in their bright, shaggy fur. In fact, they looked cute and adorable. There was no way they could sneak up and scare anyone, because they looked so cute. Also, their bright fur was easy to see from far away. So the monsters stopped trying to be scary, and decided to be friendly instead.

And that is how the monsters got their fur.

How the Honker Got His Honk

Once upon a time Honkers did not make any noise at all. In fact, Honkers liked peace and quiet so much that they chose the quietest meadow in the quietest forest for their home.

They wanted everything to be very quiet so they could read their books and do their homework, and the baby Honkers could take naps. The Honkers were very proud of all the quiet they made.

Well, one day a little Honker caught a cold. His mommy put him to bed. And that is when it happened. The little Honker blew his little nose and... "Honk! Honk-honk!"

When the little Honker felt better, his mommy let him go out to play. But every time that little Honker touched his nose, out came that nasty honk.

At first the other Honkers were polite and pretended they did not hear the little Honker honking. But the more he touched his nose, the louder his honking became. Everybody began to get angry about the noise.

Finally the little Honker decided to go into the forest by himself
until the nasty honking stopped. He walked deep into the woods
and sat down on top of a hill where he could look down on the
village below. He sat there and watched the sun set behind the
hills.

Suddenly he saw smoke rising from the town.

"Fire!" he honked.

The little Honker ran back to the village, honking all the way. "Honk! Honk!" he cried to the sleeping Honkers. He kept honking as loudly as he could.

When the Honkers saw the fire, they, too, ran honking through the village. "Honk! Honk! Honk!"

The Fire Honkers raced to the scene. In no time at all, they had put out the fire.

The Honkers could see for themselves that a honk was a very good thing to have. So they all practiced honking, and soon all the Honkers had honks of their own.

And that is how the Honkers got their honks.

ABCDEFGH